CAMP K-9

Written by **Mary Ann Rodman**

Illustrated **by Nancy Hayashi**

PEACHTREE
ATLANTA

For Nilla, who went to camp first

—*M. R.*

For Roger, best doggie ever

—*N. H.*

Published by
PEACHTREE PUBLISHERS
1700 Chattahoochee Avenue
Atlanta, Georgia 30318-2112
www.peachtree-online.com

Illustrations created in watercolor, pen, and colored pencil. Title typeset in BD Cartoon Shout; text typeset in International Typeface Corporation's Stone Informal by Summer Stone.

Jacket design by Loraine M. Joyner
Book composition by Melanie McMahon Ives

Printed and bound in December 2010 by Imago in Singapore
10 9 8 7 6 5 4 3 2 1
First Edition

Library of Congress Cataloging-in-Publication Data

Rodman, Mary Ann.
  Camp K-9 / written by Mary Ann Rodman ; illustrated by Nancy Hayashi.
    p. cm.
  Summary: Roxie is keeping a secret from her fellow campers--a blankie that she keeps hidden but wants desperately every time Lucy, a big, mean poodle, causes trouble.
  ISBN 978-1-56145-561-4 / 1-56145-561-X
  [1. Camps--Fiction. 2. Dogs--Fiction. 3. Blankets--Fiction. 4. Secrets--Fiction.] I. Hayashi, Nancy, ill. II. Title. III. Title: Camp K-nine. IV. Title: Camp canine.

PZ7.R6166Cam 2011
[E]--dc22
                    2010026687

"We're Camp K-9 pups, and we're the best!"
howl the dogs on the bus. All except me.

I have a secret to guard. It's in my Pooch Pouch,
safe in my lap.

A pug pokes her head over my seat. "My name's Pearl. What's yours?"

"Roxie," I say.

"Have you been to camp before?" Pearl asks.

"No."

"Me neither," says Pearl. "Do you think we'll get homesick?"

I shrug, and Pearl disappears. Too bad. She sounded friendly. But being friends means sharing secrets, and I can't share mine.

When no one is looking, I sniff the pouch, my secret inside. My blankie.

Wherever I go, my blankie goes, too. It makes me feel better when I'm worried or sad.

A gigantic poodle leans over the aisle. "What's in the bag?"
she growls.

"Nothing," I snap.

I want my blankie. I want it right now!

But not while that poodle's staring at me.

The bus stops.

"Camp K-9!" barks the driver. "All off for Camp K-9!"

A collie with a whistle and clipboard trots toward us.

"Roxie? Pearl? I'm your counselor, Buffy," she says.

"Let's go to our cabin. We call it the Mutt Hut."

As we hike to the Mutt Hut, I look for that poodle. She's nowhere in sight. Good.

The campers in the Mutt Hut seem like nice pups. Kia and
Rudi. Sophie and Bea. Hazel and Pearl. But what would they
say if they saw my blankie?

Bam! A big poodle paw whams open the door.

"I'm Lacy," she snarls. Her Pooch Pouch and bedroll land on my bunk.

"That's mine," I tell her.

"Mine now," Lacy sneers.

I want my blankie.
I want it right now!

"Chow Time," says our counselor, Buffy. "Lacy, put your pouch under the bench."

Lacy doesn't.

When she grabs for the steak crumbles, the pouch knocks Pearl's dessert to the floor.

"My favorite," Pearl whimpers. "Pork pudding with liver snaps."

"Sorry," says Lacy, but I know she's not.

After Snooze Time it's Pond Time.

We pair up for Splash Pals.

My pal is Lacy.

And her Pooch Pouch.

I want my blankie.

I want it right now!

At night we have Campfire. We sing
"99 Buckets of Bones on the Wall."
Buffy tells us a spooky story called
"The Haunted Mail Truck." Then, just
as she gets to the scariest part...

Ah-hooo! Ah-hooo!

Something terrible howls in the dark.

Lacy jumps out from behind a tree.

"Gotcha!" She laughs. "You big scaredy-cats!"

"Nobody calls me a cat!" snaps Kia.

"Me neither," growls Bea.

"Take it back," demands Pearl.

"Make me," says Lacy.

Nobody does.

"Bedtime," barks Buffy. "To the Mutt Hut, double-time trot."

I pant to keep up with Lacy's long legs leading the pack.

I wish that poodle had gone to some other camp.

When everyone's sleeping, I sneak out my blankie. Ahhh!

Just one little sniff and...

...the sun's in my eyes. Morning. Oh no!

I hide Blankie
under my pillow.

Today is worse than yesterday. Lacy makes trouble
all morning long.

We go for a dogtrot. Hazel trips over Lacy's Pooch Pouch.

"Sorry," says Lacy, but I know she's not.

I build a bone box
in Barks and Crafts.
Clunk! Crash! Splash!
"Sorry," says Lacy,
but I know she's not.

Next we have Game Time.

We play Shoe Chew and Bone Bury.

Frisbee and Fetch.

I wish Lacy would pack up her

Pooch Pouch and dogtrot on home.

Soon it's Pup Paddle Time. We race to the pond.

When Buffy counts us at the dock, we're missing a nose.

"Where's Lacy?" she asks.

Nobody knows. Nobody cares.

"We have to find Lacy," says Buffy.

We grumble and growl our way through the woods.

We're missing Pond Time because of mean old Lacy.

She's not in the woods,
or the chow hall,
or the crafts shed.

"To the Mutt Hut!" Buffy orders.

And there we find Lacy, sprawled on
her bunk with…

"A blankie!" I howl. "She's got a blankie!"

Now I can get even. I can laugh and call
her a scaredy-cat.

"So what?" snarls Lacy, but her nose
quivers. Her tail twitches.

Wait a minute. She's scared! She's not
really mean. She was just hiding her blankie.
Like me.

I take a deep breath.

I know what I have to do.

I ease Blankie out from under my pillow.

I wait for the others to laugh.

They don't.

"I have a blankie," barks Bea. She digs in her Pooch Pouch and pulls out a pink one.

"Me, too," squeaks Sophie.

"So do I," wheezes Pearl.

We all have blankies!
No more secrets.
Now we all can be friends.

"To the pond," orders Buffy. "Double-trot time."
Buffy counts noses. Kia and Rudi. Sophie and Bea.
Hazel and Pearl. And me and my new pal. Lacy!

"We're Camp K-9 pups, and we're the best,
north or south or east or west…"

"Best friends rock, both night and day.
Camp K-9 pups, yip yip hooray!"